Planet of the
JUMPING
BEARS

BRIAN EARNSHAW

Illustrated by

CAROLINE CROSSLAND

William Heinemann Ltd
Michelin House
81 Fulham Road
London SW3 6RB

LONDON   MELBOURNE   AUCKLAND

First published in 1990
Text © Brian Earnshaw 1990
Illustrations © Caroline Crossland 1990
ISBN 0 434 97541 9

Printed in Italy
by Olivotto

A school pack of BANANA BOOKS 37-42 is
available from Heinemann Educational Books
ISBN 0 435 00106 X

Crash Landing on Castle Rock

STAR SHIP 'WIND WANDERER' of the Intergalactic Animal Rescue Service was coming in to land on the Desert Planet.

'Out you get,' said Mum to the twins. 'This is where your Dad and I take over.'

'Aw, Mum,' grumbled Adam, who had been sitting in the pilot's seat.

'Just when we were getting there!' groaned Steffie as Dad took her place at the map video.

Wind Wanderer had just broken through the thin cloud that hid the planet's surface. Down below were sand dunes and ahead they could see Castle Rock towering up out of the desert.

Mum and Dad had taken charge because it looked like being an extra-difficult landing. Sometimes, when flying was easy, the twins, Steffie and Adam, were allowed to sit at the controls, though they were only nine

years old. But this time the star ship had to land on top of a rock with no space port and with high cliffs on every side.

'Look-outs to your places!' Mum ordered.

The twins scrambled into their look-out seats, Steffie on the right, Adam on the left.

'The top of the rock is covered with thick jungle,' Dad told them. 'If you see a clearing I want you to yell out.'

'Retro-rockets away,' said Mum. Wind Wanderer shook from end to end as the rockets fired to bring their speed down. The star ship was driven by solar wind power. It picked up these winds in the empty spaces between the stars. It only used rockets to slow down.

'Look at that rock!' Steffie gasped.

'Some pebble!' said Adam. 'Whacker Gigantico!'

Now that they were circling Castle Rock they could see for the first time how huge it was. Broken cliffs rose thousands of metres out of the desert in ledges and sheer places. It was so tall that little clouds hung around it, dropping rain into a jungle of giant rambler roses that covered the flat top of the rock. Among the branches were pink and white roses bigger than dustbin lids. As Wind Wanderer made a low pass over the rock the children could see ugly long thorns on all the branches.

'No Jumping Bears in sight, brown or grey,' Adam reported.

'I hope we haven't come too late,' said Steffie anxiously. 'Hurry up, Mum and get us down.'

Wind Wanderer was on an urgent rescue mission. Bad news had come in from a wandering space probe about the brown and grey Jumping Bears. Castle Rock on the Desert Planet was the only place on the galaxy where these two rare breeds of animal could be found. They lived there among the giant roses, drinking honey from the flowers and eating the enormous rose hip berries. But for some mysterious reason the rose hips had stopped forming and, with only dribbles of honey to keep them alive, the poor bears were starving.

That was why Mum and Dad, who were both ace Captains in the Animal Rescue Service, had been sent out in Wind Wanderer at top speed. The holds of the star ship were full of pumpkins to keep the bears alive until the roses began to grow hips again.

'A small clearing on the left!' Adam called out.

Wind Wanderer dipped, turned and hovered while Mum judged their chances of a safe landing. The fierce winds of Castle Rock shook the ship from nose to tail and lashed the thick branches of the rose jungle below them. Their wide wing-spread made ships like Wind Wanderer hard to handle and the clearing was very small.

'What do you think?' Mum asked Dad.

Dad set his jaw firmly.

'It's here or nowhere,' he frowned, 'so I say, take her down.'

'Right!' said Mum. 'Hold tight twins, we're going down.'

Steffie held her breath as Mum edged Wind Wanderer into the swaying mass of flowers and thorny branches.

'Back a bit!' shouted Adam as a sharp thorn scraped the window of his look-out pod.

'I think we've made it!' said Steffie.

But, at the very last minute, when
everything seemed fine, a spiteful gust
of wind blew out of the jungle to push
the star ship sideways. There was a
nasty rasping crash as an end panel from
the wing of Steffie's side snapped off
against a branch. Then, with a last
scraping bump! they had landed.

'Was that my fault?' Adam asked
guiltily. 'We were close on my side too.'

'Least said soonest mended,' Mum said sensibly.

'The panel has broken off clean,' Dad reported, looking out at the damage. 'If Mum gets out the pack of resin-steel bond we will have it repaired in a few minutes. Adam can help me unload the pumpkin sacks onto the anti-grav sledges. Then we will be ready to feed those bears.'

So, while Dad and Adam humped sacks out of the star ship's hold, Mum and Steffie climbed out to the broken wing tip. Steffie picked up the snapped-off panel. Then she held it while Mum gave the broken surfaces a good squirt of resin-steel. That worked like very strong hyper glue and bonded the plastic together. Then as quickly as possible they slammed the panel back onto the wing.

'Now swing on it, Steff,' her mother told her.

Steffie jumped up and swung on the wing tip. The mend held perfectly. Indeed the bond was stronger than the original plastic.

'Now for those bears,' said Mum.

Feeding Time in the Rose Jungle

THE TWO ANTI-GRAV sledges both had their full load of pumpkin sacks, but so far no one had seen nose or paw of a Jumping Bear, grey or brown. Dad thought the star ship might have frightened them, so they split into two parties. Steffie and Adam took one sledge to search the northern half of the rock. Dad pulled the other sledge to search the south. Mum stayed with Wind Wanderer to take soil samples and work out why the roses had stopped growing rose hip berries.

'Mind you don't fall over a cliff !' she warned.

'Unless you've packed a parachute,' Dad grinned.

Laughing, the twins set off.

An anti-grav sledge is easy to pull
because it always hovers an inch above
the ground. So Steffie sat on the sacks
and Adam took first turn at pulling. The
rose jungle closed around them and it
was very quiet in the green gloom.
Huge, heavily scented roses hung down
from the branches.

'Phew!' Adam wrinkled up his nose.
It's like swimming in one of Dad's
after-shave bottles!'

'But no rose hips,' said Steffie sadly. 'Poor hungry bears. Shall we try calling them?'

They stopped under a sprawling white rose tree.

'Cow-up! Cow-up! Cow-up!' Adam shouted, remembering what he had heard once on a farm.

Steffie tried:

'Cootchee – Cootchee – Cootchee!' because that worked on kittens.

Nothing happened.

'I'm going to open a sack!' Adam got out his knife. 'The smell of pumpkins might do more than all this shouting.'

He slashed a sack open, took out a big yellow pumpkin, cut it in half and laid it on the ground. They waited quietly.

'Don't look now,' Steffie hissed, 'but I spy with my little eye something beginning with J.B.'

In the branches over their heads a small brown bear with bright shining eyes had appeared. It snuffled the air and peered down at the children, clearly very interested.

'Don't move an inch,' Steffie whispered.

'What would you do,' Adam asked crossly, 'if you went into a cafe and all the waitresses sat still in the kitchen and wouldn't serve you?'

Cutting a chunk of the pumpkin he pitched it carefully up into the rose tree. A little paw shot out to catch the pumpkin chunk and in a flash the bear had gobbled it down. There was a contented growling sound. The next instant the bear made a flying leap to land with a furry 'flump!' at Adam's feet. Pumpkin was popular!

Adam cut another chunk which went

as fast as the first.

'You can see how thin he is under all that brown fur,' said Steffie. 'Let's throw lots of bits of pumpkin up into the trees.'

But there was no need. More bright eyes looked down at them from the branches. The rose trees were crowded with brown bears.

Flump, flump, flump, they came jumping down in easy gliding leaps. Soon the twins were cutting up pumpkins for all they were worth to feed the hungry animals.

'It's funny,' said Adam as he crammed pumpkin into eager paws, 'they can jump like kangaroos, but you never think of them as anything but bears.'

'They're very polite,' said Steffie, 'for bears,' she added hastily as one

extra-small bear grabbed a piece of
pumpkin almost as large as itself.

They worked away, cutting and
feeding while the bears leaped down to
line up for their rations. When all the
sacks were empty of pumpkins the twins
started to tidy up the mess and the bears
began to jump back into the rose
branches.

'Have you noticed anything funny going on?' Steffie asked with a puzzled frown.

'Like you doing some hard work for a change!' Adam suggested. He ducked quickly as his sister threw pumpkin skin at him.

'Be serious,' Steffi told him. 'Have you noticed anybody missing?'

Adam looked round, then he realised.

'No grey bears!' he exclaimed, 'only brown.'

Rooting Around for a Rescue

'RIGHT FIRST TIME,' said Steffie, 'Fifty browns but not a single grey. Yet all the books say there are the two kinds of bear. Do you think all the poor grey bears have starved to death?'

'How about asking Timber Toes here?' Adam pointed to a brown Jumping Bear that had perched on the anti-grav sledge to chew a last bit of tough pumpkin. The bear looked up as he spoke and Steffie was almost sure that it winked at her brother.

'Hey, Timber Toes,' Adam shouted loudly. 'Where are the grey bears? What have you done with them?'

The bear gave him a puzzled look and cocked its head sideways.

'Bears like you,' Steffie joined in. She pointed at the bear's furry chest, 'but . . .' she looked around for something grey.

'Like my handkerchief,' Adam butted in, and waved a very grubby handkerchief that had been white once upon a time.

Immediately the brown bear's face lit up. It flopped down from the sledge, took Steffie's hand in one paw, Adam's in another and began to tug the twins into the rose jungle. Adam ducked to avoid a big thorn and Steffie almost tripped over a long bramble.

'Do you think the bear understands?' she asked as a shower of petals as big as pillowcases fell down on them.

'If we keep going I suppose we'll find out,' said Adam. 'So long as he doesn't expect us to jump over a cliff.'

Steffie squealed. Just as Adam spoke the thick jungle growth ended and a dreadful drop opened up almost under their feet. Far far below them lay the sandy desert.

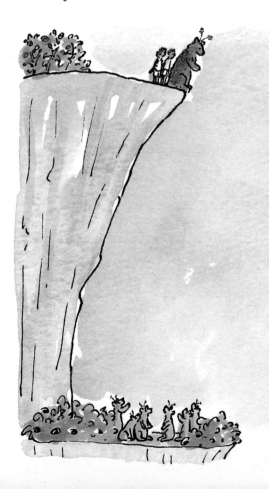

'You wicked bear,' Steffie turned to scold. But the brown bear had let go of her hand and was leaning over the edge of the cliff to point downwards.

Adam crawled gingerly to the edge and found that the top of the cliff stuck out further than the bottom. Two hundred metres lower down was a broad ledge of land covered in more giant rose trees. There in a little clearing, looking very thin and poorly, was a sad group of grey Jumping Bears.

'Grey bears,' Adam called happily. 'We've found them! They live there on a separate ledge.'

Steffie wriggled down alongside him and peeped over.

'Yes,' she said in dismay, 'but how do we reach them?'

'Let's report back to base,' Adam suggested.

The twins made their way back, pulling the anti-grav sledge behind them. Timber Toes, as Adam had called him, insisted on coming with them, perched on the sledge. Dad returned from feeding brown bears on his half of Castle Rock at the same time.

As soon as the twins told Mum and Dad about their discovery they led their parents back to peer over the cliff edge. Dad looked very grave.

'No way can we reach the grey bears down there,' he said. 'None of our ropes are long enough.'

'And we can't drop the sacks,' Mum added, 'because of the overhang.'

'Couldn't Wind Wanderer land down there?' Steffie asked. 'We must do something!'

Mum shook her head.

'Remember what the wind did when we landed up here,' she said. 'If I tried to drift in and drop a few sacks of food the gusts would catch us for sure. We wouldn't just break a wing tip. We'd smash a whole wing. That would be the end of us!'

Dad agreed.

'What we want now,' he said, 'is to root around for ideas. Let's think the problem out over a cup of tea. Bring your new friend with you,' he pointed

at Timber Toes who seemed to be listening to everything they said. 'Don't worry. We'll think of something.'

Back in the cabin of Wind Wanderer they sat gloomily drinking tea. Only Timber Toes looked cheerful. When he had turned his nose up at tea Dad had given him a whole pot of cherry jam. Steffie had disappeared into the hold where they could hear her noisily rooting about.

'Mum, did you find out why the rose hips have stopped growing?' Adam asked.

'Yes, no problem,' Mum told him. 'The rains on Castle Rock have washed one vital mineral out of the soil. The way to put the missing mineral back is to give the ground a good spray of mickadelphate. That will start the hips forming again within a week.'

'Can the grey bears last out that long?' Adam asked.

Mum looked serious.

'Some might,' she said, 'it all depends . . .'

A sudden look of shock horror crossed her face.

Steffie came staggering out of the
hold with her arms full of long metal
tubes.

'Steffie,' Mum snapped, really cross this time. 'What are you doing? Put those rockets down at once!'

'No, no no!' Dad howled. 'She might drop them. Hold steady, girl, and pass them to me, gently.'

Steffie's arms were full of the high explosive rockets that they carried to fight space pirates.

Everyone in the cabin panicked. Even Timber Toes looked upset. Steffie just grinned.

'Rockets,' she said smugly, 'rockets and steel bond! Like you said, Dad, I just rooted around and found the answer. We'll feed the grey bears using rockets and resin-steel bond!'

'Keep talking,' Mum said sternly.

'But pass me those rockets first,' Dad added. Steffie began to pass them over very carefully.

Rockets away!

'IT'S EASY,' STEFFIE explained. 'We take the explosives out of the rockets, then glue a sack of pumpkins to each rocket. Next we fly out in Wind Wanderer as close to the ledges as we dare.'

'Which won't be very close,' Mum warned.

'No matter,' said Steffie airily. 'Just as we fire a rocket at the ledge we squirt the sack with resin-steel bond. Pang! goes the rocket. Squidge! the sack sticks to the ledge. Bingo! the grey bears get the pumpkins!'

Mum and Dad looked at each other.

'You know, she might have something there,' said Mum. 'The girl's a genius!'

'With a Mum like hers,' said Dad, 'what do you expect?'

Everyone cheered up. Dad got his laser tool out and emptied the explosive heads from the rockets. Mum prepared the resin-steel.

'One thing,' Adam said thoughtfully. 'How do the grey bears get to know that the sacks are full of juicy pumpkins? Won't the rockets scare them?'

'Good question,' said Dad.

'We'll just have to take Timber Toes with us,' Steffie had the answer as usual. 'He knows about the pumpkins so he can growl the message to the grey bears.'

So it was settled. When everything was ready Mum and Dad hovered Wind Wanderer up, inch by inch, out of the clearing. They made two low passes over the jungle on top of the rock to spray mickadelphate over the giant roses. Then they dived down to the ledges for the difficult bit. That way, as Mum put it, if anything went wrong, at least there should be rose hips for the brown bears before the week was out.

Next Wind Wanderer turned on her
side and side-slipped down to hover off
the cliff as near as Mum and Dad dared
to the ledge of the grey Jumping Bears.
Fierce gusts of wind shook the star ship,
wobbling her wings and tipping her tail.
When they opened up the cabin roof to
fire rockets out, the force of the wind
was terrible. Mum and Dad wrestled
with the controls steadying the ship
while Steffie aimed her first rocket at a
tall rose tree on the ledge.

'Ready, steady, squirt!' she ordered.

As Adam squirted resin-steel on the pumpkin sack, Steffie fired the rocket.

'Whoosh!' it shot away and,

'Squidge!' it slammed into the branches.

As the smoke cleared away the whole family cheered. There, safely bonded to a branch, was the pumpkin sack.

'Now, Timber Toes,' Adam coaxed, 'pass the message on about the pumpkins.'

The brown bear's eyes shone as if he knew exactly what was wanted. He jumped onto the ship's side and sent out a long rumbling growl that echoed back from the cliff face.

'That should do the trick,' said Steffie.

'Fingers crossed,' said Mum.

For a tense minute the star ship

hovered and shook on the gale. Then the leaves below the hanging sack of pumpkins stirred. A grey furry face peered out and a bear jumped up onto the branch to which the sack had stuck. For a moment the grey bear turned towards the star ship and waved a paw. With one sharp tug, it ripped the sack open, took one pumpkin for itself and let the others tumble down to where the grey bears were gathering.

'Made it!' said Adam.

'Ready, steady, squirt!' ordered Steffie, and . . .

'Whoosh!' away shot the next rocket to leave a second sack dangling from the rose trees.

Steffie fired eight more rockets into the jungle. Only once the resin-steel failed to bond and stick onto a branch. Now the grey bears had pumpkins to

last at least a week. Whenever the winds
blew in the right direction Dad sent
another spray of mickadelphate onto the
ledge to set the hips growing again.
Wind Wanderer's task was complete.
All the Jumping Bears, brown and grey,
were saved.

The star ship soared back to the top of
Castle Rock again.

'Can't Timber Toes come home with
us,' the twins pleaded.

'Wouldn't be fair,' Mum shook her
head.

'How would you like to be the only human alone with a lot of bears?' Dad asked, and there was no answer to that.

As the star ship dropped lower and lower towards the tree tops, Timber Toes prepared to jump. He turned once to the twins and this time he really did wink. Then in one easy movement the little bear jumped down to a high rose branch and stood there looking up.

'We're going to miss you,' Adam called.

The bear waved back and then jumped down into the rose jungle.

On full thermal power Wind Wanderer soared up skywards for the long journey home.